CW00739791

Mr. Wolf and Mr. Fox 2

---

12 funny and modern fables

By the same author (on sale on Amazon):

- *Monsieur Loup et Maître Renard - 12 histoires du soir*
  mars 2022, ISBN : 979-8420346082

- *Monsieur Loup et Maître Renard 2 - 12 fables drôles et modernes*
  août 2022, ISBN : 979-8842741953

- *Monsieur Loup et Maître Renard 3 - 12 histoires du soir inspirantes qui enseignent la prudence aux enfants,*
  décembre 2023, ISBN : 979-8869993304

- *Monsieur Loup et Maître Renard - La trilogie - 36 histoires du soir inspirantes qui enseignent la prudence aux enfants*
  décembre 2023, ISBN : 979-8870220666

- *Il Signor Lupo e il Maestro Volpe - 12 storie serali*
  novembre 2022, ISBN : 979-8360679677

- *Il Signor Lupo e il Maestro Volpe 2 - 12 favole divertenti e moderne*
  novembre 2022, ISBN : 979-8362102173

- *Mr. Wolf and Mr. Fox - 12 bedtime stories*
  march 2022, ISBN : 979-8433282896

- *Mr. Wolf and Mr. Fox 2 - 12 funny and modern fables*
  september 2022, ISBN : 979-8355270537

- *Señor Lobo y Maestro Zorro - 12 cuentos para dormir*
  marzo 2022, ISBN : 979-8431569647

These books are available in paperback and ebook.

Mr. Wolf and Mr. Fox 2

———

12 funny and modern fables

Stéphane POLEGATO

Publisher: Stéphane POLEGATO
stephane.polegato.auteur@gmail.com

Print on Demand: Amazon KDP Publishing
Graphics: Flaticon, Pixabay, Canva and Microsoft Bing

Legal deposit: September 2022

ISBN: 9798355270537

To all those who encouraged me to write this volume 2,

By their words or their writings,

By sharing my posts on social networks,

By their likes,

By their reviews,

By their comments on Amazon,

And by their encouraging words that gave me wings,

Thank you!

TABLE OF CONTENTS

PREFACE   11

1. The return of Mr. Wolf   13

2. Mr. Wolf and Rebecca's chickens   19

3. Welcome to Bois du Leu!   27

4. A wolf on the frozen pond   33

5. A wolf at Christmas   39

6. Mr. Fox's friend   47

7. The wolf and the ghost   55

8. The wolf and the mouse   63

9. The wolf and the storm   69

10. The wolf cry contest   77

11. Mr. Wolf is going back to school!   85

12. The revenge of Mr. Wolf   91

The final word   99

BONUS: guide to inventing your stories   101

THANKS   111

PREFACE

This book tells the continuation of the adventures of Mr. Wolf and Mr. Fox. I advise you to read first the first volume, Mr. Wolf and Mr. Fox. But if you want to read volume 2 directly, it's possible! I just need to explain what happened in the last story of volume 1 so that you can understand what will happen now.

The last story in volume 1 was "The Land of the Happy Wolves". Mr. Fox wanted to get rid of Mr. Wolf for good. So he told him that there was a country where there were lots of big chickens to eat, the land of the happy wolves. As usual, it was a trap. Mr. Wolf thought he was going to fly to the land of the happy wolves, but he ended up in a rocket that took him to the moon and the astronauts abandoned him.

Now it's time to tell you the rest. You will finally know how Mr. Wolf was able to return to Earth. That's right! You knew he was coming back! Mr. Wolf is coming back! But he is still as naive as ever...

If you are telling these stories to your children, I encourage you to try to do two different voices for Mr. Wolf and Mr. Fox. Depending on the age of the children, it may also be useful to specify who is speaking each time (I didn't write it down each time so as not to make the dialogues too heavy).

Don't hesitate to take the time to answer your children's questions, to involve them and to listen to them. And if you think they don't know a word, take a brcak to explain it to them.

Each story ends with a moral and a proverb that you can explain to your children, taking into account their age.

If you've already read volume 1, did you get the idea to search the internet to see if Bois du Leu really existed? Well, yes! This is the neighborhood where I grew up. It is a district of the city of Sanvignes-les-Mines (in Burgundy, France) which has been razed to the ground because of the risk of collapses (underneath, there were the mine galleries). When I was writing these stories, I imagined myself in my childhood neighborhood with Mr. Wolf and Mr. Fox. Nostalgia... I take this opportunity to greet the ex-inhabitants of the Bois du Leu, especially my classmates !

Last thing: in volume 2, **you really have to read the stories in order to understand them well**. Are you ready to discover the rest ? Then good reading!

The return of Mr. Wolf

I t was already seven days that Mr. Wolf was alone on the moon when he heard a huge noise in the sky. This noise reminded him of the rocket with which he had arrived and he began to hope with all his strength, "Maybe Mr. Fox has realized that we have the wrong ship. Maybe he learned that I am alone on the moon and came looking for me!" Mr. Wolf did not know that Mr. Fox had deceived him. He still imagined that the land of the happy wolves existed and that he had just taken the wrong rocket.

Mr. Wolf was very agitated and he looked everywhere in the sky full of stars. Suddenly, he saw what he had been waiting for so impatiently: the rocket had come back for him! As soon as it landed, Mr. Wolf noticed that it was not the same rocket he had used on the way up. This one was much bigger and it had a very visible name: SpaceX.

A door slowly slid open and an astronaut stepped out of the rocket. He was wearing a beautiful white suit and a helmet that allowed his smiling face to be seen clearly. He approached Mr. Wolf and handed him an envelope on which it was written, "The return of Mr. Wolf - from Mr. Fox". How happy Mr. Wolf was! It was his friend who had written him a letter and sent him a rocket to save him! He opened the letter without delay and began to read it:

My dear friend Mr. Wolf,

You know I like to play jokes on you to teach you lessons. Well, I must confess something. I am a little ashamed of myself, because this time I went too far. I wanted to get rid of you for good and I made up that story about the land of the happy wolves to make sure you would get on the rocket. You are so naive! You should have asked me why I didn't come with you to that country where there are so many fat chickens... Sorry, the land of the happy wolves does not exist! I hope you will forgive me. Since you are alone on the moon, I have been looking for a way to bring you back to Earth. When I heard about Elon Musk and his rockets, I immediately went to him for help. He's really nice and he decided to send a rocket to bring you back. Get in quickly and the astronauts will bring you back to Earth. I'll be waiting for you at the landing and we'll go back to live in Bois du Leu[1].

Your friend Mr. Fox who wants to do you good.

In just two minutes, Mr. Wolf had learned that he had been tricked again by Mr. Fox and that the land of the happy wolves did not exist. He was sad and angry, but happy to receive this letter and to be able to go home with this rocket. After all, Mr. Fox had apologized and sent him a rocket.

---

[1] Mr. Wolf lives in France. "Bois" means "wood" in French. "Leu" (wolf) is a word in ancient French.

15

So he climbed into the rocket without hesitation, eager to get back to his friend and his wood. The astronauts gave him a suit and a helmet and he sat down on a nice chair. Poor naive wolf! He had no idea what was really waiting for him...

The journey was very long. It lasted several months. Mr. Wolf was sleeping when, all of a sudden, a strong light and loud noises woke him up. At last! He was no longer lost in this black sky full of stars. He had arrived on Earth! Curiously, the Earth was red and there was nothing: no trees, no houses, no roads... Nothing!

The SpaceX rocket landed and the doors opened. The astronauts descended one by one on the red planet in front of Mr. Wolf who did not understand anything. One of them approached him and handed him a letter on which it was written, "Welcome to the planet Mars!" Mr. Wolf opened the letter and began to read it. It was another letter from his friend Mr. Fox, who wrote this to him:

My dear friend Mr. Wolf,

If you are receiving this letter, it means that you received my first letter and that you went up in the SpaceX rocket without asking the astronauts any questions. You thought you were going back to Earth but you went to another planet, Mars! Once again, you were careless! Here you are on the planet Mars for a year. For the record, I did meet with Elon Musk, but it wasn't to ask him to bring you back to Earth right away. I knew he wanted to send people to Mars to build a city, so I asked him if he could pick up my friend Mr. Wolf who was on the moon first. He didn't want to, so I told him that you had always dreamed of going to Mars. He finally agreed and here you are on Mars! You will have to stay there for a year. Don't worry! During that time, I'll be taking care of the chickens and rabbits in Bois du Leu! I'm going to enjoy myself! Before you come back, you will have plenty of time to think about this proverb, "Prudence is the mother of safety." See you soon my dear friend!

Your friend Mr. Fox, who has fooled you again!

Mr. Wolf started to scream. He was angry at his friend Mr. Fox. Friend? Funny friend, yes! Normally, a friend is there to help us, not to send us to Mars for a year! Mr. Wolf was disgusted to have been tricked again. He thought he had become careful and experienced, but he was still as naive as ever. So he had to stay for a year on Mars and used this time to reflect on the lessons Mr. Fox had already taught him.

———

"Prudence is the mother of safety."

———

.

Mr. Wolf and
Rebecca's chickens

A fter spending a year on the planet Mars, Mr. Wolf was finally on his way back to Earth. Even though the rocket was going very fast, the trip took a long time because the journey was really long. Mr. Wolf was anxious to get back to his little wood, the Bois du Leu, and to be able to go hunting again. It had been almost two years since he had eaten a chicken! On Mars, there were none. He could only eat what the astronauts gave him, which was canned vegetables or crackers. Finally, the moment of landing arrived, "Fasten your seatbelts, we are about to land!", said the commander of the rocket.

The rocket landed in the middle of a wheat field and the door opened. Mr. Wolf jumped to the ground and began to run around the wheat field at random. This time he was on Earth, but he was lost. He remembered what Mr. Fox had written to him in his first letter, the one he had received on the moon, *"I'll be waiting for you at the landing and we'll go back to live in Bois du Leu."* So he began to yell for his friend. A few moments later, he heard screams coming from the forest next to the wheat field. He ran and entered the forest in the direction of the cries. The cries were the cries of an animal, but was it Mr. Fox? Yes! Mr. Wolf had just seen him! The two friends did not dare to come closer to each other. One was a little ashamed of having sent his friend to the moon and then to Mars; the other was a little wary and wondered if he would be able to forgive.

But the two friends were very happy to be together again and they threw themselves into each other's arms and hugged each other tightly. How good it is to be back together after two years apart! Mr. Fox began the conversation:

- I'm really sorry I lied to you about the land of the happy wolves and I beg your forgiveness!
- I forgive you, my friend! You know, at first I was very angry with you. But after a while, I thought about it, and I thought that what happened to me was a bit my fault.
- And why? asked Mr. Fox.
- Because if I had been less naive, I wouldn't have been fooled! So, it's true, you were mean, but I was stupid.
- So you forgive me?
- Of course I do! And I can tell you that I've had plenty of time to think about all the lessons you've taught me. And that's it! You'll never get me again! Now I'm careful and I won't take any more risks!
- But yes, I'm sure you've become as cunning as I am! said Mr. Fox, believing the opposite.

The two friends set out for Bois du Leu and told each other about all they had done in the past two years. Mr. Fox gave news from Bois du Leu and Mr. Wolf told what life was like on Mars. The trip took almost a month and it was very tiring for Mr. Wolf. He had eaten only vegetables and crackers for several months and had become very thin. He didn't have much strength left and could hardly walk as fast as his friend.

Fortunately for him, the two friends were approaching a village. It wasn't Bois du Leu yet, but there was probably food. At the entrance of this village, there was a nice house with a big garden. And in that garden, there was a chicken coop! Mr. Wolf felt his heart beat faster and faster. He had just heard the chickens and he could already see himself tasting them. But he had to get into the garden first. All around the house there was a big wall one meter high, and on this wall there was a fence one meter high. It was impossible to jump over it! So the two went around the house to see if there was a place to get in easily. Mr. Wolf noticed the sign on the gate:

- Did you see that sign, Mr. Fox?
- Yes! But you mustn't take any notice of it!
- What? But it says, "Bad dog"!
- And you believe everything they say?
- No, but I'm careful now! I prefer to be careful.
- That's good. But you also have to think. Look in the garden! The chickens are not locked up in the henhouse. They walk around wherever they want.
- So what? asked Mr. Wolf.

- Well, are you stupid or what? If there was a bad dog, it would eat the chickens! So that means that there is no bad dog in this house. People put up this sign to scare off thieves.
- But we are chicken thieves! So we must be afraid, right? asked Mr. Wolf.
- How funny you are! I just told you that there is no dog! So we're going to go back and get the chickens. That's all!

Mr. Fox had been very convincing but it was a trap, once again. Indeed, he had noticed that there was a doghouse at the other end of the garden. So there was a dog! It was the perfect opportunity to check if his friend had become more careful as he claimed. The two friends managed to get into the garden through the gate, which was poorly closed. Mr. Fox was wary and moved forward slowly while Mr. Wolf started to lick his lips and growl to scare the chickens before attacking them. Mr. Fox had a great idea to avoid being bitten and to get the dog to take care of his friend. He explained his plan:

- Let's split up! You go around the house to the left. I'll go around to the right. If the chickens see you, they will run away and I will be there to catch them. And if they see me, you will catch them. And then we'll share. OK?
- Good idea! says Mr. Wolf. You are really clever! I am lucky to be with you!

Lucky? Not so sure... Mr. Wolf took off running to the left, but Mr. Fox came out of the house giggling. He knew what was coming. And considering the size of the doghouse, the dog must have been very big.

Mr. Wolf finally arrived at the chickens that were pecking freely in the garden. The two hens started to cluck so loudly that the dog woke up from his nap. He weighed at least 120 lb and was a very protective dog who was friendly with both chickens. He lunged at Mr. Wolf and started biting him with all his might to scare him away. There was so much noise that Rebecca, the lady of the house, came out of the garage with a rake, "Ah, you'll see what it costs to attack my little darling hens!" Mr. Wolf had to pass by her to get out of the yard. He received a few blows with the rake and ended up joining Mr. Fox who was waiting for him a little farther on the path.

- But where were you? asked Mr. Wolf.
- Didn't you read the sign at the entrance to the house? It said, *"Bad dog"*, Mr. Fox replied.
- Yes, but you told me there was no dog!
- Did I? Then I forgot to tell you that I had seen a dog house!
- But then, why did you tell me to go around the garden? Did you know that I was going to get bitten?

- Oh, you know, you shouldn't listen to every advice! Didn't you think about it during your two years of absence?

Mr. Wolf walked away screaming. As usual, he had followed the advice of his "friend" without thinking too much. Everything seemed logical to him. Everything seemed true to him. But he had been fooled again. It wasn't so bad because it was a lesson to him. He had just learned that those who give us advice do not always try to help us.

———————

"The advisers are not the payers."

———————

3

Welcome to

Bois du Leu!

M r. Wolf and Mr. Fox arrived at Bois du Leu on a beautiful winter day. Mr. Wolf was very happy. He commented on everything he saw:

-   Look! The pond is all frozen and there is snow on it!
-   Yes, it's winter, said Mr. Fox.
-   Oh, look how beautiful the two fir trees are with all that snow! But they look like they've grown, don't they?
-   Yes, they sure have, a lot has happened in two years.

Mr. Wolf rolled around in the snow and laughed. How good it was to be home at last! He started to run towards the school. The small hill, a right turn, a left turn, and he soon arrived in front of the school. The students were in class with their teacher. Mr. Wolf laughed as he thought back to the day he had gone to school with the other students and thought it would be fun to do it again. Mr. Fox interrupted him:

-   Aren't you hungry?
-   Oh yes, I am! I'd like to eat a chicken. I haven't eaten one for so long!
-   Sorry, but it's going to be very complicated!
-   Ah, why? asked Mr. Wolf.
-   The farmer was tired of wild animals attacking his chickens. He replaced the fence on his chicken coop with a fence that is higher. So it will be difficult to get over it.

Mr. Wolf was so hungry that he decided to go see anyway. The two friends approached the chicken coop slowly so as not to be spotted by the farmer's big dog. The fence was higher, but it didn't seem as strong. So Mr. Wolf had an idea:

- I will try to make a hole in the fence with my teeth!
- But how are you going to do that? asked Mr. Fox.
- I'm going to crunch the fence and pull with all my strength, to the right, then to the left.
- If I were you, I wouldn't do that, my friend!
- Don't worry! I'm not the stupid little wolf you once knew. I have become very strong and very smart. Everything is going to be fine!
- Well, do as you wish, but I would have warned you!

Mr. Wolf could not believe it. His friend had become a real coward. He walked proudly up to the fence, turned to his friend to wink at him, and bit down on the fence. "Wow!!!" he yelled. "Ouch!!!" He could feel an electric current running through his entire body. It hurts like crazy! His muscles were all tense and he couldn't let go of the fence. It was as if his teeth were stuck to the fence by the power of electricity. Mr. Fox looked at him and laughed and did nothing to help him. After a while, there was a loud noise, like a firecracker, and the electricity stopped. Finally, Mr. Wolf was able to catch his breath and he asked Mr. Fox for an explanation:

- But what happened?
- You bit an electric fence, my friend!
- And what made you laugh?
- It was funny to see you with all your hair up. Ah ah ah! I told you to be careful.
- Because you knew it was an electric fence?
- Yes, look at the sign above your head! It says, *"Danger: electric fence"*.

Mr. Wolf was angry. He thought his friend had become a coward. He thought he was going to impress him. But in the end, he had been fooled. Those who think they are strong are in danger because they tend not to listen to advice.

So Mr. Fox was right: it had become very difficult to eat chickens at Bois du Leu! But fortunately for Mr. Wolf, his friend was clever and he had an idea.

- I know where to find chickens! said Mr. Fox.
- Ah! And is it safe?
- Yes. I think so. Since we can't catch Erick the farmer's chickens, I'll take you somewhere else. Follow me!

Mr. Fox led Mr. Wolf past a store that had just opened at Bois du Leu. The store had a little bit of everything: bread, candy, fruits and vegetables, but mostly meat! Mr. Wolf asked:

- Is that where you think you'll find chickens?
- Yes! said Mr. Fox. There are plenty of chickens in this store. You just have to go in and help yourself.
- But isn't it dangerous? asked Mr. Wolf.
- No! Not at all! It's very easy! But I understand, you are afraid! You don't want to do it because you are a coward!

Mr. Wolf was very embarrassed. Indeed, he was very afraid. He remembered the many times he had followed Mr. Fox's advice and it had ended badly. But at the same time, he didn't want to look like a coward. So he hesitated a lot and thought, "I'll go. No, it's dangerous, I'm not going! And then yes, I'm going. I'm going. Oh no! I can't." Meanwhile, Mr. Fox continued to mock him:

- Forget it, you're too small. You're not strong enough! If you're scared, too bad! We won't eat chickens today.
- Stop saying that, I'll go! replied Mr. Wolf.

Without thinking, he slipped into the store, trying to be discreet. He soon arrived at the meat department and was very surprised to see chickens without feathers and wrapped in plastic. These chickens did not move at all, so it was very easy to catch them. All he had to do was to get out quickly to finally enjoy the food. Unfortunately for him, some customers had noticed him and had gone to the front desk to report that there was a dog in the meat department (because people thought it was a dog). A tall man approached Mr. Wolf. He was wearing a T-shirt that said "Security" on it. In his hand he had a large stick with a collar on the end. With a quick and precise motion, he put the collar around Mr. Wolf's neck and squeezed so hard that Mr. Wolf could not move and choked. Mr. Wolf was led to a van. He barely had time to speak to Mr. Fox:

- You told me it was safe and easy. You liar!
- You should have listened to your instincts instead of listening to me. One should not always listen to the advice of others!

Mr. Wolf didn't have time to answer. The man pushed him into the van and took him to a shelter where there were many abandoned dogs. All these dogs looked unhappy because they were locked up in cages. The man gave Mr. Wolf to a lady who worked at the shelter. When she realized that it wasn't a dog, she stepped back and shouted, "But it's a wolf!" The man then grabbed a stick and began hitting Mr. Wolf, who ran away screaming. When he saw that he was alone and safe, Mr. Wolf thought to himself, "I think I have a long way to go. I swear I will never listen to Mr. Fox again!"

———————

"Young people listen easily to bad advice."

———————

A wolf on the
frozen pond

Mr. Wolf had returned to Bois du Leu after running away from the shelter. It was winter and very cold. Everything was white, or almost white, because of the frost and snow. Even the pond at Bois du Leu was covered with snow! If it wasn't for the little wall around the pond, you wouldn't have known there was a pond. The children were at school and the parents were at work. Meanwhile, Mr. Wolf was walking around the neighborhood looking for food when he met his friend Mr. Fox and said:

- Hi Mr. Fox! How are you doing?
- Oh, I'm doing great! How are you? I heard you got hit with a stick again?
- Yes, and it's your fault! I'm better, but I'm bored and hungry! I don't know what to do.
- So come with me to the Bois du Leu pond! We'll go sliding on the frozen pond!
- Oh, really! The pond is frozen? But isn't it dangerous to slide on it?
- No, it's not! Come on, come with me!

Mr. Wolf didn't look very reassured but he followed his friend to the pond. It was really beautiful! Everywhere the snow was full of footprints of the locals, except on the pond. No one had walked on the frozen pond yet. So the snow was like a nice white coat on the pond. Mr. Wolf immediately noticed the large sign that had been placed in a prominent place at the edge of the pond. It showed a picture of the frozen pond with children sliding on it. Mr. Fox didn't even look at the sign. He was already sliding on the lake! He was going back and forth and laughing a lot. He called out to his friend:

- Come on, let's go sliding!
- No! I don't think that's very safe. You should stop.
- But why? I am having fun and there is no danger. What are you afraid of?
- I think the ice might break and you will end up in the icy water!
- You are such a coward! said Mr. Fox as he got out of the pond.

Mr. Wolf was naive and often reckless, but he was also quite fearful when he found himself in an unusual situation. And walking on the frozen pond was really unusual for him! He was more used to coming to the pond to drink water or to swim on a hot day. So he showed the sign to Mr. Fox and asked him:

- Why do you think they put up a sign with children sliding on the frozen pond?
- To explain that you can go sliding, of course! said Mr. Fox.
- But then, why is the picture crossed out with a big red cross?
- It's to scare us! They don't want us to go sliding! But I assure you, there is no danger! I did it well, and you saw, the ice did not crack!

Mr. Wolf really didn't want to go on the frozen pond. He had understood the sign and knew there was danger. He should have stopped listening to Mr. Fox who was trying to convince him to do something reckless. But sometimes, when you know you shouldn't do something, you still want to do it. And Mr. Wolf really wanted to slide...

Mr. Fox was clever and he was not short of ideas to convince his friend. So he tried to change his friend's mind by telling him:

- You don't want to go because you are afraid. You're a coward and you're not a bold person!
- I am not a coward! And what's a bold person?
- A bold person is someone who is bold.
- And what is boldness?
- Boldness is the fact of daring to do difficult things or new things. For example, if you were a bold person, you would cross the frozen pond by sliding!

Mr. Wolf was now torn: he was afraid, but he didn't want to look like a coward. And besides, he thought, if Mr. Fox could slide, he should be able to slide too. Suddenly he remembered that his friend was always setting traps for him and that they always ended badly. So he told him:

- I understand! You're talking about daring me to cross the pond and end up in the icy water.

- But no! If it was that, I wouldn't have been sliding across the pond. Think about it! Haven't you ever heard the saying, *"Fortune favors the bold"*?
- No. What does it mean?
- It means that you have to cross the pond if you want everything to succeed in your life!
- Really? said Mr. Wolf in astonishment.

Mr. Wolf was still fearful, but he was changing his mind. His friend had just convinced him. He forgot about the sign. He forgot about the danger. He forgot about caution and climbed over the wall onto the frozen pond full of snow. As he still seemed to hesitate, Mr. Fox encouraged him by repeating: *"Fortune favors the bold! Fortune favors the bold!"* Mr. Wolf didn't really understand this proverb, but he wanted to be bold. He didn't want to be a coward and he didn't want Mr. Fox to laugh at him. So, he jumped on the pond and made long slides. He was so happy and proud that he shouted, "Look at me, Mr. Fox! I'm sliding! I'm sliding down the frozen pond! See, I'm bold!"

But suddenly, the ice began to crack. Mr. Wolf stopped moving. He tried to reach the edge of the pond slowly, but he was too heavy and he disappeared under the ice that had just broken. He found himself in the frozen water and swam to the edge of the pond, but under the ice. Mr. Fox heard him knocking under the ice and removed the snow to see him. Mr. Wolf was trapped: he couldn't get out of the icy water. Mr. Fox hit the ice with all his strength with his four paws but the ice was too solid. He had to find a solution quickly! As luck would have it, there was a very large rock right next to the pond, under the sign. Mr. Fox grabbed this very large rock and threw it with all his might onto the ice. The ice broke and Mr. Wolf caught the very large rock on his head. He finally managed to get out of the water, but completely frozen and with a huge bump. He barely had the strength to complain:

- See, I told you it was dangerous and not to go on the frozen pond!
- Yes, it was very dangerous, admitted Mr. Fox. And you shouldn't have listened to me. You are much heavier than I am, that's why the ice broke with you and not with me. The next time someone challenges you and tells you that you're not bold, you should be wary and stay safe! It may be a trap or a foolishness. In some situations you need to be brave, but in others it is better to be cautious.

"The art of being both very bold

and sometimes very cautious is the art of success."

A wolf at Christmas

Christmas Day was approaching. It was still hard to hunt for our two friends, Mr. Wolf and Mr. Fox. The chickens were kept warm and the rabbits hardly came out of their burrows. It was urgent to find food. Mr. Fox had an idea and explained it to his friend:

- Do you know what humans do on Christmas Eve?
- No. Do you?
- Yes, they have a nice meal before they go to bed.
- And what do they eat? asked Mr. Wolf.
- Only good things! Anyway, I know there's turkey.

Mr. Wolf began to dream. He had heard of turkeys before, but he had never eaten one. Mr. Fox had told him that they were even better than chickens, so he hoped to have some for Christmas. Yes, but how do you get into people's homes without being spotted and beaten? Mr. Fox was having fun because he knew his trap would work. His plan was to send his friend to the farm on Christmas Eve to get hit by the farmer. So he explained:

- I know how we could eat good food on Christmas Eve.
- Ah? said Mr. Wolf. How?
- Well, the children are looking forward to Santa Claus because he's coming to bring them

presents. All you have to do is pretend to be Santa Claus and go to the farmer's house for Christmas Eve dinner.

- Oh, and you think I'll get to eat some good stuff?
- Yes, you will! You'll love it!
- But what about you? Aren't you going to eat anything?
- Yes, I will! I can stay outside, near the window of the house. When you get home, you can open the window and pass me lots of good things. Then you can run outside and we'll share!

Mr. Fox knew that, one way or another, this would end badly for his friend. Mr. Wolf was so naive that he almost never saw the pitfalls. When Christmas Eve came around, Mr. Fox had found a Santa suit and gave it to his friend. Mr. Wolf looked really good in red with his fake white beard! Just before entering, Mr. Wolf received some advice from Mr. Fox:

- Be nice because Santa is nice! And start all your sentences like the real Santa.
- Okay, but what do you say then?
- You have to start all your sentences with, "Oh-oh-oh!"
- Oh oh oh! Okay! replied Mr. Wolf who was proud to have understood.

Mr. Wolf knocked on the farmhouse door. Colleen, the farmer's wife, came to open the door and was very surprised to see Santa Claus at dinner time.

- Santa Claus! What a surprise! You came early this year. Where is your sleigh?
- Oh oh oh! I left it in the forest.
- And the presents? Where are they?
- Oh oh oh! They are in the sleigh, my little one!
- OK, says Colleen. Would you like to eat with us, Santa? We were just about to eat.
- With pleasure! Uh... Oh oh oh! With pleasure!

Mr. Wolf couldn't believe it. Nobody had noticed that he wasn't the real Santa Claus! Well, apparently... He was going to get to eat some good stuff. He grabbed two chicken legs, opened the window and handed them to Mr. Fox, who was there. Mr. Fox whispered, "Two chicken legs? Is that all? Go back and get the turkey and let's get out of here!" But Mr. Fox knew that would be too difficult for Mr. Wolf and that was part of his plan. As expected, Mr. Wolf wanted to stay a little longer. He thought, "Why just take the turkey and run? It's great to celebrate Christmas with family!" He was so happy to be surrounded by children. He thought, "I'm going to eat as much as I can and then take off my costume to scare the kids!" Colleen invited everyone to the table and suggested that Santa say a few words before the meal began:

- Santa, this is the first time you're having Christmas dinner with us. Can you tell us a few words about the North Pole?
- Oh oh oh! I don't know that place.
- How funny you are, Santa! This is the place where you live!
- Ah? Oh oh oh! But yes, I was joking!
- Another question: to do your job, you must love children a lot, right?
- Oh oh oh! Yes! I like to sca... Uh... Yes, I like them a lot, said Mr. Wolf who stopped just in time (he was about to say that he liked to scare them).

Finally, the meal began. Mr. Wolf had completely forgotten his friend who was waiting for him at the window. He ate a lot, especially the turkey! He thought it was delicious and had seven servings. Everyone was amazed at how much he ate; and Colleen thought, "No wonder he has such a big belly!" He even tried the cheese. He took six pieces with bread and ate five pieces of the chocolate log that Colleen had made. At the end of the meal, the children offered him chocolates. The poor guy didn't know not to eat too much of the good stuff! He ate so much that chocolate was dripping from his lips and he also tasted the little cookies prepared by Jace, Colleen's son. When the meal was over, everyone went to bed. Colleen kissed him to thank him for having spent the evening with them and said:

- You can rest a little in the armchair next to the fire. When it's midnight, you can go and get the presents and put them under the tree, as usual. Good night and good luck, Santa!
- Yes. Uh... Oh oh oh... said Mr. Wolf who was now very tired.

Mr. Wolf should have left quickly since there was nothing left to eat, but he wanted to stay a little longer. He thought, "I'm going to rest for a while; then I'll take off my costume and go scare the children in their rooms!" But his stomach hurt so much and he was so tired that he fell asleep in the chair. Bad luck for him, there was a very observant child in that house! Jace, the farmer's son, thought it was strange that Santa Claus came to eat at their house on Christmas Eve. He knew that the real Santa had to be very busy that night. So he had watched and listened to him a lot during the meal, and he had seen that it was a wolf in disguise. He had seen his tail hanging out behind his Santa suit. So he got up shortly after going up to his room and came up behind the soundly sleeping Mr. Wolf to give him a little lesson. Jace grabbed the wolf's tail and gently moved it into the fire in the fireplace. The tail caught fire and Mr. Wolf woke up screaming, "Ouch! It hurts! It burns!" And he ran out of the house screaming in pain. Jace came out of the house to look at him. He saw Mr. Fox still standing under the window, laughing as he watched Mr. Wolf burn. It was really funny! It looked like fireworks going off in the forest! Jace barely had time to ask the fox his name:

- What is your name?
- My name is Mr. Fox. What's yours?
- Jace!
- Merry Christmas Jace! said Mr. Fox as he ran away.

Mr. Wolf finally stopped running and rolled in the snow to put out the fire. His tail was all black and smelled like toast. Mr. Fox came up to him and lectured him:

- This time, you've been fooled by yourself, my friend!
- Yes, I guess I should have listened to you for once! I should have taken the turkey and gone to eat it in the forest with you.
- Yes! You were too greedy!

———————

"You can't overindulge in good things."

———————

Mr. Fox's friend

E veryone had a very merry Christmas at Bois du Leu, except Mr. Wolf. Sure, he had a great meal, but he had a burned tail and a really bad stomach. For several days, he didn't move from his den. He didn't even want to eat anymore! He spent all his time thinking about the last lesson he had learned, *"You shouldn't overindulge in good things."*

Meanwhile, the snow continued to fall. Jace, the farmer's son, loved to play in the snow and wanted to go play in the woods. But his mother was very protective and forbade him to go out for fear of the wolf. She had seen the wolf run away from the farm on Christmas Eve and was afraid it would take revenge by eating her little Jace. But Jace didn't always obey. So he put on his boots, jacket, gloves and hat, and sneaked out of the farmhouse.

Since there was no school that day, he would have time to play in the snow for a long time. Jace was a brave boy and he was not afraid of wolves. So he began to sing a well-known song, "Let's go for a walk in the woods while the wolf isn't there. If the wolf were there, he would eat us. If the wolf isn't there, he won't eat us!" And the wolf wasn't there since he no longer came out of his den because of his stomach ache. But what Jace didn't know was that he wasn't alone in the forest...

Suddenly, Jace heard the sound of a branch breaking, as if someone had stepped on it. He turned around, but no one was there. Jace stopped singing and started making a snowman. When he finished making the big ball for the belly and the little ball for the head, he looked for pieces of wood to make the nose, eyes and mouth. Once again, he heard noises. He immediately thought that it was his mother who had come to get him and he shouted, "Mommy, is that you? Mommy? Is anyone there?" But no one answered. Jace continued to look for pieces of wood, thinking it must be an animal noise.

When Jace had found all the wood he needed, he went back to his snowman and noticed footprints that were not his own. It was an animal, but which one? So Jace began to ask:

- Is there a wolf here?
- No! said Mr. Fox, pointing to himself (he was hiding behind a bush). It's me!
- Oh, hello Mr. Fox! How nice to see you again! We had a good laugh on Christmas Eve, didn't we?
- Oh yes, Jace! You really got it right! I have a feeling you're as naughty as I am.
- Yes! I like to make jokes. How about you?
- Me too! I always make jokes to Mr. Wolf!
- That's great! If you want, we can try to play a joke on him together, Jace suggested.
- Good idea! replied Mr. Fox.

Jace seemed to forget that he was talking to a wild animal and Mr. Fox forgot that he was talking to a child. The two talked like friends and laughed and made up all sorts of jokes:

- Tying Mr. Wolf to a chair in the schoolyard so that the children would stick out their tongues and laugh at him.
- Locking Mr. Wolf in the henhouse so that he gets beaten by the farmer.
- Give him chocolates made with toothpaste and pepper.
- Giving him a rabbit trap without explaining how it works so he'll get his legs stuck.

And there were many other jokes like that. After a while, Mr. Fox had a great idea:

- I've got it! I'll tell Mr. Wolf that you're playing in the forest and he'll want to come out and scare you. He'll probably want to bite you in revenge because you burned his tail.
- Great! And you can make him think he's going to trick me! But in the end, we'll set him up.
- Okay! said Mr. Fox. Let me do it. I've got an idea!

Mr. Fox ran to Mr. Wolf's den and said:

- Mr. Wolf! Get out of your house quickly! I just saw the little boy who burned your tail on Christmas Eve! He's playing in the forest and he's alone!

- What? All alone?
- Yes! Come quickly!
- I'm going to catch him and bite him!
- Unfortunately, I think you won't be able to catch him. I've seen him run and he runs faster than you!
- So quickly, come up with an idea!

Immediately, Mr. Fox gave him an idea: dig a hole on the path to the farm, put leaves on it and wait for the boy to fall in and bite him. Mr. Wolf wanted to move so fast that he didn't take the time to think. He didn't think about what he had learned, *"Don't confuse speed with haste."* He asked for clarification:

- How do you make sure the boy falls into the hole?
- It's easy! Just make the hole big enough and deep enough. When the child passes through, he will inevitably fall in.

Mr. Wolf had been so angry since Christmas Eve that he immediately set out to dig. With all his might, he scratched the earth with his four paws and dug his hole at full speed. Then he covered the hole with leaves as Mr. Fox had advised and waited. He was ready to pounce on Jace. But Jace did not come. While Mr. Wolf was digging his hole, Mr. Fox went back to Jace and told him:

- Mr. Wolf is digging a hole to trap you. I gave him the idea! He's going to put leaves on it and he thinks you're going to fall in the hole on your way home.
- I know what we can do! said Jace. You can lure the wolf to another part of the forest by telling him I'm there. Meanwhile, I'll go to his hole and stand right behind him.
- Good idea, Jace! That's what I wanted to tell you. And then I'll tell him I saw you running towards your house.
- That's great! We'll have a good laugh!

As planned, Mr. Fox lured Mr. Wolf into the middle of the forest and Jace went home looking for the leaf-covered hole. It was so easy! Mr. Wolf had made a big hole and put leaves on it without realizing how weird it looked. On the path, there was only snow. So a pile of leaves in the middle of the path, it was too obvious! Mr. Wolf was always so naive...

While Jace was settling down behind the leaf-covered hole, Mr. Fox told Mr. Wolf that he had just seen the child running towards his house. Mr. Wolf rushed to his hole. When he got to Jace, Jace started to run as well to pretend to run away. Mr. Wolf was in such a hurry to get revenge that he didn't notice the pile of leaves on the path and fell into his own hole!

He wanted to make sure the boy couldn't get out of the hole, so he dug a pretty deep hole. Jace and Mr.

Fox came up to him and laughed at him. Then they left him in his hole and walked away laughing.

———————

"Whoever digs a hole for someone

is likely to fall in it himself."

———————

The wolf and the ghost

Finally, spring arrived. This was great news for Mr. Wolf and Mr. Fox! It meant that the little animals would come out of their burrows more often and it would be much easier to hunt.

One day, Mr. Wolf had eaten well. The hunt had been very good and he had a full belly. He decided to take a little nap in the field next to the Bois du Leu school. It was a beautiful day. Everything was going well for him.

Suddenly, he was awakened by the cries of children. He had forgotten that the children were out in the yard at recess. The children were playing, shouting and running around. Mr. Wolf spoke to himself, "What a racket! I'll calm them down!" He began to shout, thinking, "They'll be afraid of me and run back. I can finish my nap in peace." But the noise continued...

Mr. Wolf got up and moved closer to yell at the children to make sure he scared them. What he heard made him angry. The children were playing wolf. One of them had just touched one of his friends and he shouted, "You're the wolf!" The wolf ran after all the other children who were laughing. When he touched another classmate, he too shouted, "You're the wolf!" Mr. Wolf felt that the children were laughing at him. They were acting as if they were not afraid of wolves! He thought, "Ah, you want to make fun? Let's see if you don't get scared!!!" And he began to howl as he put his big hairy paws on the fence of the school wall, "Ooh!..."

The children stopped running and making noise and looked toward the wall. They saw Mr. Wolf's head sticking out over the wall and they all started laughing and rolling on the floor. One could hear them:

- How funny!
- Another clown in a wolf costume!
- I'm sure it's a joke from my father!

And all the children laughed a lot. Then everyone stopped laughing and looked at Mr. Wolf. The shouting started again and the children began to play wolf again. Mr. Wolf was surprised and really angry. He decided to go talk to his friend about it. When he arrived at Mr. Fox's house, he told him what had just happened. Mr. Fox gave him an explanation:

- I'm sorry for you, but you have to understand.
- Understand what? asked Mr. Wolf.
- Well... For two years, you weren't there. The children came to believe that there were no more wolves in Bois du Leu. Their parents promised them there would never be again. And they believed them!
- Ah, the rascals! But you should have seen how they laughed when they saw my face!
- Yes, I understand, it must not be funny for you, said Mr. Fox.

- Not funny at all! I'm upset that I don't scare kids anymore!!!

Mr. Wolf continued to tell what had happened. He repeated the same story several times. That's what angry people often do. Meanwhile, Mr. Fox was thinking. He wasn't really listening. He was thinking of a plan to play a bad joke on his friend. And as usual, he quickly came up with an idea! He stopped Mr. Wolf, who was still repeating that the children had laughed at him, and he explained his idea:

- Stop! I have an idea!
- Ah? An idea to scare the children?
- Yes! The children are not afraid of you anymore, but I know who they are still afraid of.
- Who? asked the wolf.
- Ghosts!!!
- Oh, and what's a ghost?

Mr. Fox explained to him that ghosts didn't exist, that the children were very afraid of them and that they looked like transparent people who were scary. Mr. Wolf got even angrier:

- What? Children are afraid of ghosts and ghosts don't exist?! That's not fair! I exist, and they are not afraid of me anymore!
- Don't worry! said Mr. Fox. I have an idea. You are going to become a ghost!

- Oh? And how are we going to do that?
- Well, you're going to dress up as a ghost and go scare them at school.
- All right! I'm going to have fun!

Mr. Fox told him how to look like a ghost. They had to hide under a white sheet so that they wouldn't be seen. For several days, the two friends searched for a white sheet. One day, they finally saw one on the clothesline of Colleen, Erick's wife. Mr. Fox grabbed the sheet, put it on his friend and asked him to try to scare him. Mr. Wolf yelled:

- Ooh!
- No! said Mr. Fox. You must not howl like a wolf! You must do the cry of a ghost!
- But how does a ghost sound?
- I don't know, but you mustn't howl like a wolf! Try a higher pitch instead.

Mr. Wolf practiced for a few minutes and finally got a scary scream that sounded like a ghost scream (even though ghosts don't exist). Now it was time to go to school. Mr. Wolf was already imagining the scene. He was going to enter the school very slowly and rush into the classroom doing his ghostly scream. The kids and the teacher were going to get the fright of their lives! He was super happy to be able to do this and was already thanking Mr. Fox:

- Thank you so much for giving me this idea! I'm going to have fun scaring the kids and the teacher!
- Please, it's normal for friends to help each other!

Once he arrived in front of the school, Mr. Wolf hid under his white sheet and tried to move forward. But since he couldn't see anything, he asked his friend for help. Mr. Fox made two small holes for him and said:

- All you have to do is look through these little holes. Remember, you have to make a ghostly scream. Have fun!
- Thank you! I'm a bad ghost, said Mr. Wolf as he laughed and walked into the school.

When he arrived at the classroom door, he prepared to make his scream and opened the door slowly. With his two small eyeholes, he couldn't see much, but that didn't stop him from making his scream. Strangely enough, no one shouted. He then decided to take off his sheet to try to scare them as a wolf. He was very surprised because there was no one there and the shutters were closed. But a strange thing happened: the classroom door opened and closed several times with a slam. It was Mr. Fox who wanted to teach him a little lesson and who had also hidden under a white sheet! Mr. Fox came into the classroom screaming and said, "I am a ghost and I am going to eat you!" Mr. Wolf was very scared because he thought it was a real ghost. He ran to the exit door and ran like he had never run before! Mr. Fox was proud of himself. He had pulled off a good joke and decided to reassure his friend and explain what had happened:

- So Mr. Wolf, were you able to scare the children and the teacher?
- Oh no! There was no one there and it was dark. And I can tell you that you are wrong, ghosts do exist!
- No, they don't! replied Mr. Fox.
- Yes, they do! I saw one in the classroom and it was terrifying! He even said he wanted to eat me! Luckily, I managed to save myself.

Mr. Fox explained to him that the reason no one was at school was because it was Saturday, and that he was the one dressed up as a ghost to scare him. He took the opportunity to remind him of a little lesson he had already taught him.

———————

"Such is tricked who believed to trick."

———————

The wolf and

the mouse

A few days later, Mr. Fox was worried that he would never see Mr. Wolf again in the forest or anywhere else in the Bois du Leu area. So he went to his house and called him:

- Mr. Wolf, are you there?
- Yes, I'm in my den!
- Come with me, we will hunt together today!
- No! I don't want to leave my den anymore.

Mr. Wolf was still in shock since he had seen a ghost at school. He had the fright of his life. Normally, he was never afraid. He was not afraid of anything. But since that day, he was afraid of ghosts. Mr. Fox tried to reassure him:

- But I told you I was the ghost! I was dressed up like you, with a white sheet!
- Maybe, said Mr. Wolf, but I'm afraid of ghosts now!
- Oh, don't be so stupid! I told you that ghosts don't exist!
- Are you sure?
- Yes! Come on, come with me!

Mr. Wolf finally decided to go out to hunt, but he was different. Usually, he walked with confidence, as if he was the king of the Bois du Leu. He was not afraid of anything and all the animals would run away when they saw him coming. Now he was shy and walked close to Mr. Fox; and he looked around as if he was afraid a ghost would jump out at him. Suddenly he heard a little noise behind a bush. It must have been a small animal hiding, but Mr. Wolf was very frightened and started to run home at great speed. Mr. Fox followed him and went into his den with him. He asked him why he had run away:

- Did you see a ghost and run away so fast?
- No, but I heard a noise and I got scared!
- So you are afraid of ghosts and what else now?
- I don't know. And I don't know why I was afraid, but I was afraid.

It's often like that with people who are afraid. They're afraid of one thing, then two things, then three... And often they're afraid of things that don't exist, like ghosts, or things that exist but don't hurt.

Mr. Fox was worried about his friend. He liked to play jokes on him, and he laughed when Mr. Wolf got hit with a stick, but it made him sad to see him so afraid. He said to himself, "You have to treat evil with evil." meaning that he wanted to scare Mr. Wolf so he wouldn't be scared anymore. He had already shown him that there was no point in being afraid of ghosts because they don't exist. Now it was time to show him that there was no need to be afraid of the little animals that wander around in the forest.

Since Mr. Wolf was still hiding in his den and didn't want to come out, Mr. Fox went back to the middle of the forest to hunt. He saw a careless little mouse nibbling on a mushroom. He quietly approached it and grabbed it by the tail. The mouse immediately began to beg him:

- Oh, please, Mr. Fox! Don't eat me! I am too young to be eaten. I just ate a mushroom and it makes the meat taste bad. I'm sure you don't like mushrooms, do you?
- Don't worry little mouse! I have other plans for you!
- Oh? And what do you want? I'll do whatever you want, but please don't eat me!
- I told you, I won't eat you. But I would like you to help me heal my friend.
- Oh? Is your friend sick?
- Yes, in a way.
- And what kind of disease is he?
- He's afraid of ghosts and I think he's afraid of small animals now. I'd like to let you loose in my house and I'll bring him to my house so you can scare him. Then I'll explain to him why he doesn't have to be afraid of you, and he'll probably be cured.
- Okay! And then you'll let me go?
- Yes, of course I will!

Mr. Fox went home and let go of the little mouse, threatening, "If you run away, I will find you and eat you!" Of course, the mouse was so scared that it didn't move. Then Mr. Fox went to Mr. Wolf's house. Mr. Wolf didn't want to go out hunting. So Mr. Fox said to him:

- I knew you wouldn't want to hunt, so I went hunting by myself and caught two rabbits. Come with me, I invite you!
- Okay, but let's not stay outside for long because I'm scared!

When the two friends arrived at Mr. Fox's den, he let Mr. Wolf go in first. When the mouse saw the wolf, it was very frightened and started to scream. Mr. Wolf thought that the mouse was screaming because it wanted to attack him and he was even more afraid than it was! He ran out of the den and shouted:

- There's a mouse, there's a mouse in your den!
- Yes, said Mr. Fox. But it's a very small mouse. Why are you afraid?
- I don't know. Maybe because it screamed?
- You don't have to be afraid. This mouse is very small and it should be afraid of you. Go to it and scare it!
- I don't dare! said Mr. Wolf. I am too afraid!
- Come on! You have to dare. If you dare, you'll see that you won't be afraid anymore and that it was ridiculous to be afraid of such a small animal.

Mr. Wolf thought for a while and said to himself that it was probably a good idea to listen to his friend. He hesitated, however, because he remembered all the times he had listened to him and it had ended badly for him. Finally, he found the courage to go back. He counted to motivate himself, "One, two, three!" And he went into the den, screaming to scare the poor little mouse. The little mouse scurried away from the den and was never seen again in the forest of Bois du Leu. Mr. Wolf came out of the den very happy and thanked his friend Mr. Fox for helping him overcome his fear. For once, he had done the right thing by listening to him. And for once, Mr. Fox's lesson was not too painful for Mr. Wolf.

———————

"Courage grows by daring and fear by hesitating."

———————

The wolf and the storm

T he next morning, Mr. Fox came to get Mr. Wolf to go hunting with him. Mr. Wolf immediately agreed to come out of his den and boasted to his friend:

- You know, I'm not afraid anymore. I have become a fierce wolf again and I am not afraid of anything!
- Bravo my friend! So you are not afraid of ghosts anymore?
- No! You know very well that ghosts don't exist. You're the one who taught me that.
- That's good! replied Mr. Fox. And you're not afraid of mice either?
- No! It's the mice that should be afraid of me. I'm not afraid of anything anymore, I tell you!

As they walked through the forest, Mr. Fox heard little noises all around them. He watched Mr. Wolf for his reaction. Mr. Wolf didn't even notice the noise. He really didn't seem to be afraid anymore. Mr. Fox pointed out to him that there must be some small animals hiding:

- Didn't you hear those noises?
- Yes, I did! It must be mice or other small animals hiding in the bushes.
- And that doesn't scare you?
- No, it doesn't! How many times do I have to tell you? I am cured: C.U.R.E.D! I am not

afraid of anything anymore! Do you understand?

- Okay, okay... Great!

Mr. Fox was happy for his friend. Deep down, he liked this wolf. He had met him when he was very small, when he was still called Wolf Junior. And it was he who had taught him to hunt. Mr. Wolf had become big and strong, but he still wasn't very smart. In fact, he was still quite naive. He listened to bad advice and didn't listen to good advice. So Mr. Wolf was cured. He was no longer afraid of anything.

Mr. Fox was wondering what trick he could play on his friend when he heard the storm roar in the distance. Since Mr. Wolf had arrived at Bois du Leu, there had not been a storm yet. So he didn't know what it was and asked his friend:

- Mr. Fox, did you hear that loud noise?
- Yes, it must be the storm.
- And what is the storm?
- What! You've never seen a storm in your life?
- No, I haven't. Tell me what it is, please.

Mr. Fox tried to describe to him what a thunderstorm was in simple words. He explained that there was rain, wind, loud noises and sometimes lightning flashing across the sky. He added that lightning sometimes fell on the ground and that it could start a fire. He told of the beauty of lightning and the power of lightning. Hearing all this, Mr. Wolf felt as if his heart was melting like candle wax and his legs began to shake. His hair stood on end and he began to shake and ask:

- But what should we do? It looks very dangerous!
- But no, don't worry! The storm is far from here and nothing will happen to us.

Just then, a flash of lightning crossed the sky above their heads. It was an impressive flash. Mr. Wolf started to run towards his den when he heard the sound of thunder. He asked his friend:

- What's that big noise?
- That's a dragon screaming to scare you! said Mr. Fox, chuckling.

Mr. Wolf was terrified again and fled back to his den where he felt safer. He was exhausted from all the emotions of the day and quickly fell asleep. The next morning, Mr. Fox came to pick him up to go hunting. Mr. Wolf did not want to go out because he was still afraid of the storm. His friend encouraged him by telling him that the storm was over and that there was no need to be afraid. When he refused to go out, Mr. Fox laughed at him:

- You're a scared little boy! You're the wimpiest wolf on earth! And maybe even the most fearful animal in the world!

72

- No! said Mr. Wolf. I am not afraid!
- Yes, you are! You are afraid and you have no courage!
- That's not true! I am very brave and I am not afraid of anything!
- So come out of your hole and hunt with me if you are not afraid of anything!

Mr. Wolf was afraid but he didn't want to admit it to his friend. He preferred to be seen as a brave and strong animal rather than as a coward. So he went out and hunted with his friend.

It was still a gray day. It was windy and dark clouds were in the sky. The rain was beginning to fall when a thunderclap was heard. Of course, Mr. Wolf was very scared but he didn't want to show it. He was tired of being called a coward by his friend. A flash of lightning shattered the sky and there was another thunderclap. Mr. Fox was surprised to see that his friend was not afraid anymore. So he asked him:

- Mr. Wolf, did you see that lightning?
- Yes... Nothing serious...
- Yes, it is! It's very dangerous! said Mr. Fox. Come on! We can't stay here! We have to get to safety quickly!
- Well, go home if you are afraid! I am not afraid and I am brave, very brave!

Mr. Fox insisted that Mr. Wolf take cover. He reminded him that lightning can sometimes turn into fire and strike very hard. But Mr. Wolf wanted to look strong and brave. He wanted to impress his friend and he even thought that Mr. Fox was making up the story about lightning and fire. So he said, "Well done, the lightning turning into fire! But you mustn't take me for a fool. I'm not that naive!"

Mr. Fox realized that it was useless to insist. He ran home, leaving his friend alone in the middle of the meadow where they had had their discussion. It was raining harder and harder and the storm was still rumbling. Mr. Wolf was a little afraid that lightning would strike him. So he decided to take shelter under a big tree, which you should never do in a storm...

A lightning illuminated the whole sky and, unluckily, the lightning fell right on the tree which was used as shelter by Mr. Wolf. The tree was crossed by an immense electric current and caught fire. As Mr. Wolf was leaning on the tree to avoid the rain, the electric current passed through him and he caught fire. He ran towards the Bois du Leu pond to put out the fire, but the lightning struck him a second time and he passed out. Luckily for him, Mr. Fox had just come out of his house and asked him to stop fooling around and come to safety. He managed to put out the fire and dragged Mr. Wolf to his den.

The next morning, when Mr. Wolf woke up, he smelled like he was toast and hurt all over. His hair was black and his head was spinning. Mr. Fox lectured him and said:

- See, I told you it was dangerous and you had to get out of the way!
- Yes, you were right. But I thought you were making fun of me and I wanted to be brave.
- What happened? asked Mr. Fox.
- Well, when you left, it was raining really hard and I wanted to take shelter. I saw a big tree in the middle of the meadow and thought it was a good idea to put under the tree.
- Ouch, ouch, ouch! You'll know it now. When it's stormy, there are lots of things you shouldn't do.

Mr. Fox continued his lesson by explaining all the things not to do in a storm. He also took the opportunity to explain all the things you should do to avoid getting into trouble. In any case, what is sure, it is that one should not be smart with the storm!

"Fear does not avoid danger, neither does courage."

I encourage you to take some time to emulate Mr. Fox by explaining to your children what not to do in a storm.

And to make sure you don't forget anything, you can check out this article:

https://www.rd.com/list/things-never-do-in-thunderstorm/

The wolf cry contest

For several weeks, Mr. Wolf didn't dare to show his face because he was ashamed of his black and burnt hair. With time, new hair grew and he became as beautiful as before. Spring had just ended and it was already the end of the school year for the students of Bois du Leu. To celebrate the beginning of the vacations, the party committee decided to organize a contest for the first time. It was the wolf cry contest! All over the neighborhood, and even in the woods, there were posters announcing the contest:

The whole neighborhood was buzzing with wolf calls for days. Everyone wanted to win the first prize: a helicopter ride over Bois du Leu! The children practiced their wolf-like screams, "Whoo! Ooh!..." At first, the parents were annoyed by the wolf-like screaming, but they all started howling because they wanted to win the helicopter ride too.

Just then, Mr. Wolf decided to come out of his den. He was surprised to hear all the screaming and ran to Mr. Fox to tell him the good news:

- Mr. Fox! Do you hear that howling?
- Yes, those are wolf howls.
- Finally! said Mr. Wolf. It's certainly my family. I'm going to see my parents and my brothers again.
- Let's go see! said Mr. Fox, who didn't quite believe it.

When the two friends arrived near Erick's farm, they heard the beautiful howling of a wolf cub coming from inside the house. Mr. Wolf wondered why this young wolf was in the house and called out to him. The young wolf answered him by howling in the same way. Mr. Fox had already understood but Mr. Wolf always understood a little later. So he exchanged a few more howls before he understood. Unfortunately for Mr. Wolf, it wasn't a wolf from his family. It was the boy who had burned his tail at Christmas. He realized this when he saw Jace at the window waving to his friend Mr. Fox. It upset him to see this child reminding him of that sad time in his life.

He continued walking through the neighborhood and heard more wolf howls. All the children and adults in Bois du Leu were howling instead of talking. Some were howling while walking, others while driving or working. It was really nonsense! Mr. Wolf became angry when he realized what was going on. After seeing a poster of the wolf cry contest, he asked Mr. Fox what a helicopter was. Mr. Fox explained:

- It's a machine that flies, kind of like a rocket. But don't worry, it's not for going to the moon or Mars!
- And it's to take a ride on this thing that they all make wolf calls, right?
- Yes, that's what it says on the poster. It's for a ride over the Bois du Leu. It must be beautiful from above!
- So I'll do the helicopter ride! shouted Mr. Wolf.

For once, he had a huge advantage over everyone else. He was a real wolf! He didn't need to learn to howl like a wolf because he had been doing it since he was a little boy. It was his instinct to howl and he did it very well.

Mr. Fox advised him to practice to make sure he would win, but he refused, saying that he was already sure he would win and that it wasn't worth the effort. Besides, it was summer and very hot. Mr. Wolf was having trouble breathing and asked his friend for help:

- Mr. Fox, I'm too hot and can't breathe, tell me what I can do to make it better!

- Go to the Bois du Leu pond. At the far end of the pond, you will see a fisherman who has installed a fan. All you have to do is stand next to the fan and you'll be able to breathe better with the fresh air.
- Thank you for that! That's a great idea!

Mr. Fox had just set a trap for his friend again. Mr. Wolf had no idea and spent the whole afternoon with his head right in front of the fan. Meanwhile, Mr. Fox took the opportunity to meet his friend Jace at the farm and gave him some advice on how to do his wolf calls. Mr. Fox was not a wolf but he was often with Mr. Wolf, so he knew very well how to do the wolf call. Jace listened to him very carefully because he knew he still had a lot of progress to make and he really wanted to win this helicopter ride.

The next day was the day of the contest. Everyone, absolutely everyone spent the morning screaming for practice. It was really painful for Mr. Wolf to hear all that yelling. He thought, "What a bunch of losers! I'm the best. I'm going to win this contest for sure!" Mr. Fox had encouraged him to be a little more humble and to practice, but he preferred to sit in front of the fisherman's fan.

When the time came for the contest, everyone was gathered at the Bois du Leu pond. The festival committee asked everyone to stand on a platform and give their shout in front of everyone. Each time someone made his wolf cry, everyone applauded, even if it was a very small cry, not very loud and not very pretty. The last one to pass went up to the stage after listening to some more advice from Mr. Fox. It was Jace, the farmer's son! He screamed so loudly and so well that everyone applauded much louder than for any of the other candidates. The chairman of the party committee spoke up and said:

- I think we will all agree that we just heard the most beautiful wolf howl in all of Bois du Leu, right?
- Yes!!! said all the inhabitants of the village.
- No! said Mr. Wolf.

But nobody had heard it because of the many claps. He thought he had to hurry if he wanted to win the contest and take the helicopter ride over Bois du Leu. So, without thinking too much, he jumped on the stage and started screaming. Well... he tried to yell. He couldn't do it anymore and his throat was very sore. He tried several times to make his scream to impress everyone and to scare them at the same time. But no sound came out! Nothing at all! Some of the dads picked up rocks and threw them at him to scare him away. Amused by the situation, all the children in the village did the same. Mr. Wolf had to run away at full speed. He had just been taught a lesson in humility.

As usual, he went to his friend Mr. Fox to ask him what had happened. Mr. Fox explained that he had sent him to the fan because he had been a naughty and hadn't wanted to prepare for the contest. He told him that he shouldn't stay too long in front of the fan because he could catch a cold. He explained that Jace had won the contest with his help. While Mr. Fox was teaching him the moral of the story, a helicopter flew overhead and they saw Jace waving at them. Mr. Wolf screamed with sadness and said:

- I wanted to do that helicopter ride!
- Yes, but you were too sure of yourself! said Mr. Fox. You boasted. That's what happens when you think you're too strong!

———————

"Pride goes before the fall."

———————

11

Mr. Wolf is going

back to school!

The day after the wolf cry contest, Mr. Wolf started to think seriously and he told himself that things had to change. He was more than tired of being tricked and never making the right decisions. This beginning of the year had been difficult for him. He had been afraid of a ghost, then afraid of a mouse and finally afraid of the storm. He had also been humiliated at the wolf cry contest. Everyone laughed at him and laughed when he tried to howl but couldn't. He had grown big and strong, but he was still reckless and naive, and he still wanted to grow in wisdom and gain experience. He decided to go to Mr. Fox for advice. Mr. Fox was taking a nap against a tree. Mr. Wolf woke him up and said:

- Good morning, Mr. Fox!
- Ah! Good morning, my friend. You've got your voice back, I see?
- Yes, it's better. But I'm still angry. And I really wish I was smart and clever like you!
- Well, you just have to go to school!
- Very funny! I'm not going to do it again! The schoolmaster won't leave me alone.
- But I'm not talking about the children's school! I'm talking about the school for animals.
- Oh, there's an animal school?

Mr. Fox told him about the school where he had gone when he was a little fox. It was there that he had learned to read and count and had learned to be very cunning. Mr. Wolf imagined himself learning and becoming careful and cunning. He said nothing to his friend, but his intention was to become more cunning than he was so that he could set traps for him.

Mr. Fox suggested to Mr. Wolf that he go and see this school. There was only one small problem, and that was that this school was not in Bois du Leu. The animal school was in Verne Wood. It was about an hour's walk to get there. Mr. Wolf took the opportunity to ask some questions:

- Are there only animals in this school?
- Yes. Even the teacher is an animal. She's a bear.
- Ah? And she is nice?
- Yes, with those who are good and work well, she is very nice. Don't worry!
- And how long do I have to go there to be clever like you?
- I don't know. The teacher will tell you.

The two friends arrived in front of the school. There was no one there because it was also the big vacation for the animals. But fortunately, the teacher was still there. She was pleasantly surprised to see Mr. Fox through the window and came out to talk to him:

- So Mr. Fox, do you want to go back to school?
- No teacher! I came to show a friend the school.
- What is your name?   the teacher asked Mr. Wolf.

- Uh... My name is Mr. Wolf.

The teacher was impressive when she stood on her two back legs. Mr. Wolf was not very comfortable and he was a little afraid of her. After taking all the information, the two friends returned to Bois du Leu. On the way, Mr. Fox asked his friend:

- So, do you still want to go to school?
- Yes, but I hope the teacher will be nice.

The summer passed quickly and it was already the first day of school. At Bois du Leu, all the children went to school while Mr. Wolf went to the animal school at Verne Wood with Mr. Fox. Mr. Fox gave him some advice and let him go in alone. The teacher greeted all the students with a smile and then told them in a very stern tone:

- Sit down and shut up! I'm going to explain the rules of the school to you! It is forbidden to speak without asking permission by raising your hand! It is forbidden to move around! It is forbidden to copy on your neighbor!...
- Teacher! Can we go drinking without asking permission? asked Mr. Wolf.
- Who dared to speak without raising his hand to ask permission?
- Me! answered Mr. Wolf shyly.

- Well, you'll be an example! Get up and go to the corner! That's what happens in my class when you don't respect the rules!

Mr. Wolf got up and went to the corner. The teacher asked him to put his paws on his head and turn around. This was a very bad start for him! A little later, the teacher handed out presentation cards to the animals. They had to write their parents' names. Mr. Wolf thought back to the day he got lost in the big forest. It made him sad for the rest of the day.

When the school day was over, Mr. Wolf went home. Mr. Fox had come to pick him up and asked him:

- So, did you have a good day at school?
- No! I was punished and sent to the corner because I talked without asking permission. And I didn't like the teacher's lessons!
- Oh? And what lessons were there?
- We did mental arithmetic, reading, spelling and dictation. It's useless! I don't want to go back!
- Come on, my friend! You shouldn't give up so quickly. You still have a lot to learn to become as smart as me!

Mr. Wolf was not very convinced but he went back to school the next day. He was scolded because he tried to eat one of his classmates, a rabbit. He copied his neighbor, the turtle, and was denied recess. Finally, he started to scream in the middle of a moral class when the teacher explained that he had to be nice to all the other animals in the class. He didn't want to be nice to them. He just wanted to eat them all!

At the end of this second day of school, Mr. Wolf was very tired and especially very disappointed. He decided to stop going to school and went to tell Mr. Fox:

-   I will not go to school anymore! I will learn to be careful and cunning on my own! And soon, I'll be the one to play jokes on you, you'll see!
-   As you wish, Mr. Wolf! But don't think you'll learn better on your own!

———————

"He who teaches himself may well have a fool for a teacher."

———————

The revenge of

Mr. Wolf

So Mr. Wolf decided to quit school and try to become more cunning himself. He was really fed up with being tricked by his friend Mr. Fox and was thinking more and more about getting revenge. Of course, it's not very nice to get even, but Mr. Wolf thought that a little lesson wouldn't hurt his friend.

The day Mr. Wolf was afraid of ghosts, Mr. Fox tried to reassure him that it was normal to have certain fears. He even said that everyone has at least one fear and that some people prefer to hide their fears so they won't be laughed at. Mr. Wolf thought about this and said to himself, "So that means Mr. Fox has at least one fear too!" This pleased him. He imagined his friend running or making a funny face because he was afraid, and that made him laugh.

From that day on, Mr. Wolf occupied his days with only two things: hunting for food and watching Mr. Fox. He watched him carefully to try to figure out what he was afraid of, but Mr. Fox didn't seem to be afraid of anything. After a few days, Mr. Wolf asked his friend:

- Tell me, do you remember when you told me that everyone has at least one fear?
- Yes, very well!
- I was wondering what fear you had.
- I'm not afraid of anything, except spiders! If I see one, I panic, scream and run away!
- Okay! replied Mr. Wolf, smiling slightly.

Mr. Wolf was very happy because he had finally figured out how to play a joke on his friend. This was the first time Mr. Fox was going to be tricked and scared. All day long, Mr. Wolf looked for a spider. There are lots of them in the forest, but he didn't want a small spider. He wanted a big spider with legs full of hair. When he found it, he grabbed it and ran to Mr. Fox. He called to him to come out of his den:

- Mr. Fox, come out! I have a surprise for you!
- I'll be right out! That's nice, I like surprises!

When Mr. Fox came out, Mr. Wolf threw the big spider at his feet. Mr. Fox understood why his friend had asked him what he was afraid of. He grabbed the spider without being afraid, ate it and said to his friend:

- Thank you! I like to eat spiders!
- But you weren't afraid! said Mr. Wolf.
- No! It was a joke. I am not afraid of spiders.
- You lied to me! If you were a real friend, you would tell me what you are afraid of.
- Yes, I admit, I lied to you because I was ashamed to tell you the truth. In fact, I'm only afraid of dolls.
- Are you serious? You're afraid of dolls?
- Yes! I can't even look at them!

Mr. Wolf assumed that this time his friend was telling the truth. So he went in search of a doll. It was easy enough to find, but he had to be able to take it without being spotted. So he waited until nightfall and sneaked into a house through the window. He took a large doll, thinking it would probably scare Mr. Fox more. The next morning, he was excited because he knew he could finally scare his friend. He called out to him:

- Hey, come here! I have something to show you!
- Another surprise? said Mr. Fox as he walked out.
- Yes, the surprise is hidden behind me. Can you guess what it is?
- A chicken?
- No!
- A rabbit?
- No, a doll! said Mr. Wolf, laughing.

Unfortunately for him, Mr. Fox also laughed. This was the second time he had lied to him. Mr. Wolf reproached him:

- You have laughed at me again! You are no longer my friend! I am leaving!
- Wait, Mr. Wolf! This time, I am really going to tell you the truth. I have only one fear. It's the fear of water!
- You're lying! I know you go swimming at the Bois du Leu pond when it's hot.

- Yes, but I always stay at the edge to keep my footing. I never go in the middle of the pond because I can't swim.
- Ah? said Mr. Wolf in surprise.
- Yes. I didn't learn to swim because I almost drowned when I was a little fox. Since that day, I am afraid of water!
- Is this true? So you do have a fear?
- Yes. But it's not so bad.

Mr. Wolf had his revenge. But as he wanted to be sure to succeed, he spent a few more days thinking. It was simple: all he had to do was take Mr. Fox to the middle of the pond! After thinking about it, Mr. Wolf decided that the pond wasn't deep enough. If he really wanted to scare his friend, he had to take him to the sea. So he went to find him and said:

- I'd like to go on vacation by the sea. Do you want to come with me?
- Oh yes, I would! I'd love to.

Mr. Wolf was proud of himself. His friend had no idea. He didn't understand what was going to happen at the sea. When they got to the beach, Mr. Wolf suggested that they take a little boat ride. Mr. Fox agreed because he had no idea what was going on. They both got into a boat and started rowing out to sea. When they were very, very far from the beach, Mr. Wolf pretended to see something in the water and said,

"Oh, look at that big fish!" Mr. Fox bent down to look and Mr. Wolf pushed him into the water!

Finally! After all these adventures, for the first time, Mr. Wolf had managed to trick Mr. Fox. He was super proud of himself and laughed as he watched his friend struggle in the water. But Mr. Fox was so cunning that he had planned it all. From the beginning, he suspected that his friend wanted to take a boat ride to knock him into the water. In truth, he could swim very well, but he had said he couldn't swim to teach his friend a little lesson. He was struggling to make it look like he was going to drown. He was calling for help:

- Mr. Wolf! Mr. Wolf! Help!
- What? I didn't hear right! I didn't hear well! Mr. Wolf answered him.
- Help me, my friend! Or I will drown!
- First tell me if you are afraid!
- Yes, I am very afraid!
- And how does it feel to be fooled? How does it feel to be tricked?
- Oh! I'm sorry for all the jokes I've been playing on you. I'm sorry! Help me!

Mr. Wolf took pity on his friend and held out his paw to get him back into the boat. Mr. Fox pulled with all his strength on Mr. Wolf's paw and made him fall into the water. He climbed into the boat and began to move away. Mr. Wolf realized that he had been tricked again and shouted:

- Let me into the boat!
- No! You wanted to make me fall in the water, so you will swim back!
- Come on! Let me in! If I swim back, I will have to swim for at least three hours!
- Too bad for you! While you're swimming, you'll have time to reflect on the proverbial, *"He who laughs last will laughs best!"*
- I'll get you, Mr. Fox! One day I'll get you!
- Yes, maybe! But until then, look behind you! I think you should swim a little faster if you want to see me again one day! See you soon Mr. Wolf!

Mr. Wolf looked behind him and saw sharks. Decidedly, he was always so naive and imprudent.

———————

"He who laughs last will laugh best."

———————

The final word

If you liked it, please tell others about it!

And if you'd like to say thank you and give me some encouragement, you can do so with a comment on Amazon so that everyone can benefit.

If you write a nice review of the 2 volumes,

Mr. Wolf and Mr. Fox will be very happy!

If you'd like to write to me, here's my address:

stephane.polegato.auteur@gmail.com

If you haven't read volume 1, Mr. Wolf and Mr. Fox - 12 bedtime stories, what are you waiting for? It's just as good as this one!

Photo taken on February 23, 2022 at Bois du Leu, at the site of the missing school. I was writing the first volume of the adventures of *Mr. Wolf and Mr. Fox*.

Photo taken on April 22, 2022 with *Monsieur Loup et Maître Renard*, the french version of this book.

BONUS: guide to inventing your stories

To help you make up your own *Mr. Wolf and Mr. Fox* stories, I'll first explain how I get that imagination and write. Then I'll let you come up with ideas by guiding you to bring your imagination to life.

1. How do I make up my stories?

a) <u>Find the problem</u>:

As you may have noticed, every story has a problem, a trap or a joke. Since Mr. Wolf is always getting tricked, we have to come up with problems that he will encounter. Sometimes I take time to try to come up with them, but most of the time I get my ideas during the day. So I'm on the lookout for new problems that might happen to Mr. Wolf. I often get ideas while talking to someone, watching a movie, walking around, washing dishes, on the subway, etc.

Whenever I get an idea, I write it down in my phone. I created a document in Google Drive so I always have access to it. Even if the idea isn't great, even if I tell myself that it might be complicated to write a story about it, I write it down. From time to time, I look at all the ideas I've had and think about them.

Not all of my ideas are good, or I would have already written volume 3! But some are. Sometimes a great idea comes to me and I write a story immediately. Sometimes it takes a few days for my idea to become a great story. Sometimes I don't have an idea for several days or weeks. But sometimes I have a vivid imagination for a few days. So I take notes.

It is very important to take notes! The best ideas don't necessarily come when you're at your computer writing a story or putting the kids to bed. They can come when you wake up from a busy day at work or at any time of the day. If you don't write it down, you may forget it forever. So, we take notes!

b) <u>Find a moral and a proverb</u>:

I just talked to you about writing down ideas for problems, traps or jokes. Now let's talk about the moral of the story and the proverb. I like to end my stories with a moral and a proverb. Do you think I write the story first and then look for the moral and proverb? Or is it the other way around? Well, it depends! Sometimes I get an idea for a trap, it makes me laugh and I start to imagine what will happen. I try to find the moral and the saying before I start writing the story. But if I can't, I go ahead anyway. I set the scene and set the trap. During the writing process, the moral of the story becomes obvious and easy to write. What's more complicated is sometimes finding a proverb that fits the story.

To find suitable proverbs, I use the same technique I use for problem ideas: I take notes. Every time I think of a proverb or hear one (if you're paying attention, you'll hear quite a few), I write it down on the same Google Drive document. I don't know if I could use that proverb, or for what story it might work, but I write it down.

From time to time, I look at my document with my list of problems and my list of proverbs. Seeing these problems and proverbs sometimes gives me inspiration. Then I look forward to having some time to write and I enjoy it!

c) <u>Find advice to give to children</u>:

I have yet another way that I recommend. Sometimes I don't look for proverbs, but I do look for ideas for advice to give to children. What to tell them to warn them of danger? What safety tips to give them? For example, I want to tell them to beware of people who give advice. I think it's important to teach them that they should listen to advice but not be naive. They need to know that some people give advice without wanting to benefit us, or even wanting to harm us. I then try to find a story to illustrate this fact and I look for a moral and a proverb. That's how I came up with the second story in this book, with the following proverb, *"The advisers are not the payers."*

2. What do proverbs teach us?

I think it is important to explain the role of proverbs to children. So I encourage you to take time to talk about proverbs at the end of each story. Children may memorize some proverbs. Some may think that proverbs apply in all circumstances and at all times. But there is nothing magical about a proverb!

I'll give you an example to show what I think you should be careful about. One of the proverbs that illustrates my type of story is: *"Such is tricked who believed to trick."* This proverb is said to warn someone who would like to set a trap or harm someone else. By saying this proverb, we are giving a warning: you want to do harm, it could well turn against you! But there is nothing automatic about it. Some people do harm and don't get caught. They set traps and don't fall into them! Life is not governed by proverbs...

I hope you understand what I mean. As parents, we want the best for our children. We give them cautionary advice to avoid certain pitfalls. And we hope they will remember our advice when they have to make choices. I told my children these stories to empower them to act wisely. I also wrote them down to share with you for the same purpose.

Now here are some ideas to help you make up (or write) Mr. Wolf and Mr. Fox stories with the same intent.

3. Find problems!

To find problems, sometimes you just have to start a sentence and it comes by itself. I'll give you an example and let you find others:

Mr. Wolf does something stupid:

- ○ He bites a policeman (make up the reason).

- ○ ....

- ○ ....

- ○ ....

- ○ ....

- ○ ....

- ○ ....

- ○ ....

- ○ ....

Mr. Wolf is afraid of (think of animals, situations, emotions, people, objects...) :

- Girls
- ....
- ....
- ....
- ....
- ....
- ....
- ....
- ....

Mr. Fox makes Mr. Wolf believe that :

- Wolves can go to the movies for free.
- ....
- ....
- ....
- ....
- ....
- ....
- ....

4. Find cautionary proverbs!

I suggest you try two methods. First, try to remember proverbs that could go with our type of stories. You will probably find many of them already. Write them down in a notebook or on your phone (it's handy because you always have it with you). You can reuse the ones from my two books.

Then, I suggest you go fishing for proverbs on the internet. Depending on the problems you found, you may have an idea of the kind of proverb you need. I have often started a story and needed a proverb to illustrate the moral of the story.

Ex: If I need a proverb that shows that you should think before you listen to advice, I go on the internet and search for "proverb advice". Many proverbs will be too long, too complicated or inappropriate. But I will surely be able to find a good and quite famous one.

It's up to you! I'll let you find proverbs (if they are related to the problems and fears you found, even better!) :

- ○ ....
  ....
- ○ ....
  ....

o   ....

    ....

o   ....

    ....

o   ....

    ....

o   ....

    ....

5. Find tips to give to children!

Now, I'm sure you have plenty of ideas! So why not jot them down here (or on your phone) to use for stories. For now, don't come up with a story. It's too hard to do everything at once. Just write down the tips you want to convey.

I'll give you an example and let you continue:

o   Never follow a stranger on the street, even if they promise you candy!

o   ....

    ....

o   ....

    ....

- ○ ....
  ....
- ○ ....
  ....
- ○ ....
  ....
- ○ ....
  ....

6. Get started!

In Volume 1 and Volume 2, I gave you tips and ideas for making up your Mr. Wolf and Mr. Fox stories. Now I encourage you to get started!

Remember, we are all capable of making up stories! Some will be great, some will be good, and a few will be a little less good. Don't let that discourage you! If your kids love stories, don't deprive them!

And if you really can't make up stories and your kids are begging for them, write to me to encourage me to write volume 3!

THANKS

I would like to thank all those who read the first volume of the adventures of *Mr. Wolf and Mr. Fox*. It encouraged me a lot to continue. When I ended the first volume, I left Mr. Wolf alone on the moon and wrote: *"But don't worry too much about Mr. Wolf. He will be back soon..."* Thanks to those who told me they were waiting for the sequel and wondered how Mr. Wolf would ever get back to Earth. This motivated me to write this volume 2.

Thanks to **Panda Grenouille** for his drawing of Mr. Wolf (illustration of the story n°1) and to his son **Marius** for his nice drawing and for his little word.

I am a self-published author and my book is not available in bookstores. So I'm very grateful to everyone who gave me a review on Amazon and who told their friends and family about my book (either verbally or via social media). Please continue to do so! Thank you!

Finally, thank you to **my parents** who are promoting my book to their friends. That's cool, keep it up!

Greetings to my American friends who probably recognized their first names in my stories: Colleen, Erick and their son Jace. Hello also to their other children: Roman, Bethany, Selah. Greetings from Paris!

Stay in touch!

My Instagram and Facebook accounts are in French (yes, I am French) but you can write me in English. I read and write English.

On Facebook:

https://www.facebook.com/stephane.polegato.auteur

Click on "Add" to subscribe to my page. You can also click on "Review" to recommend me. Thank you!

On Instagram:

https://www.instagram.com/stephane.polegato.auteur

Click on "Subscribe" to subscribe to my page. You will be informed if I publish another book.

Author page on AMAZON:

Visit my author page to see the books I have published (in French, English and Spanish).

Volume 3 (the sequel to the series) was published on Amazon in December 2023.

In Volume 3, it's Mr. Wolf's turn to make a new friend. Thanks to her, he can play a few jokes on his friend Mr. Fox. But Mr. Fox won't stand for it. If he perseveres, perhaps Mr. Wolf will finally succeed in tricking his friend. He who laughs last, laughs hardest...

Sur Amazon, il existe aussi la trilogie qui comprend les histoires des 3 tomes (3 livres pour le prix de 2).

If you liked my book,

please go to **Amazon**

and leave me

a good review and rating!

Thank you so much!

Legal deposit: September 2022

Printed in Great Britain
by Amazon

36949051R00067